Jāzeps Osmanis
Secret

Illustrated by Ingrīda Pičukāne

Translated by Žanete Vēvere Pasqualini & Kate Wakeling

A modern nursery rhyme from Latvia #007

Dearest Mum, come over here,

and Dad can be
all-ears.

But my sister mustn't know this secret

and to my brother: DO NOT LEAK IT.

17

Don't breathe a word,

21

So Mum, please won't you promise me?

23

— Um...
— Funny thing is, I can't recall...

Solve the puzzle!

Find the letters!

1.	2.	3.	4.	5.	6.	7.	8.	9.

Dear friends!
You must find the word hidden in this book. It's the Latvian word for "secret"...

letter by letter

1. What letter is on Grandpa's helmet? (p.11)
2. What letter can you see on the bubblegum bubble? (p.5)
3. How many kids are there in the yard? (the first letter of the number) (p.17/18)
4. What letter is hanging from the sister's necklace? (p. 14)
5. What letter can you spot in the bubblegum scraps? (with a line on the top) (p.6)
6. What is written on the kid's orange t-shirt? (p.15)
7. What letter can you see on the brother's chair? (p.13)
8. What is the third letter on the shopping bag? (p.2)
9. What letter is formed from the scooter's smoke? (look at the page in the mirror, turning it upside down) (p.9/10)

answer: autumn

This book was published with the support of the Latvian Literature platform together with the Ministry of Culture of the Republic of Latvia and the Latvian State Culture Capital Foundation.

First published in the UK in 2020 by the Emma Press, Birmingham, UK
Originally published in 2013 as "Noslēpums" by Liels un mazs, Riga, Latvia

Text © Jāzeps Osmanis, 1963
English-language translation © Žanete Vēvere Pasqualini and Kate Wakeling, 2020
Illustrations © Ingrīda Pičukāne, 2013

BICKI-BOOKS
Artistic director – Rūta Briede
Design – Rūta Briede and Artis Briedis

Printed in Latvia by *Talsu tipogrāfijā*
on *Munken Pure* 150 gsm and *Munken Pure* 300 gsm

A CIP catalogue record of this book is available from the British Library
All rights reserved.

ISBN 978-1-912915-49-1